I0452227

The Haunted Book

Elaine Wiley

Illustrations by Luther Lomax

Copyright © 2022 by Elaine Wiley.

ISBN   Softcover   978-1-952750-34-2
        Ebook   978-1-952750-35-9

All rights reserved. No part of this book may be reproduced or transmitted in any form or by any means, electronic or mechanical, including photocopying, recording, or by any information storage and retrieval system without express written permission from the author, except in the case of brief quotations embodied in critical reviews and certain other non-commercial uses permitted by copyright law.

1

On Halloween, which was my birthday, my sister Marissa and I decided to have a slumber party.

It was a dark and stormy night, with rain pouring heavily and the drops hitting the windows loudly.

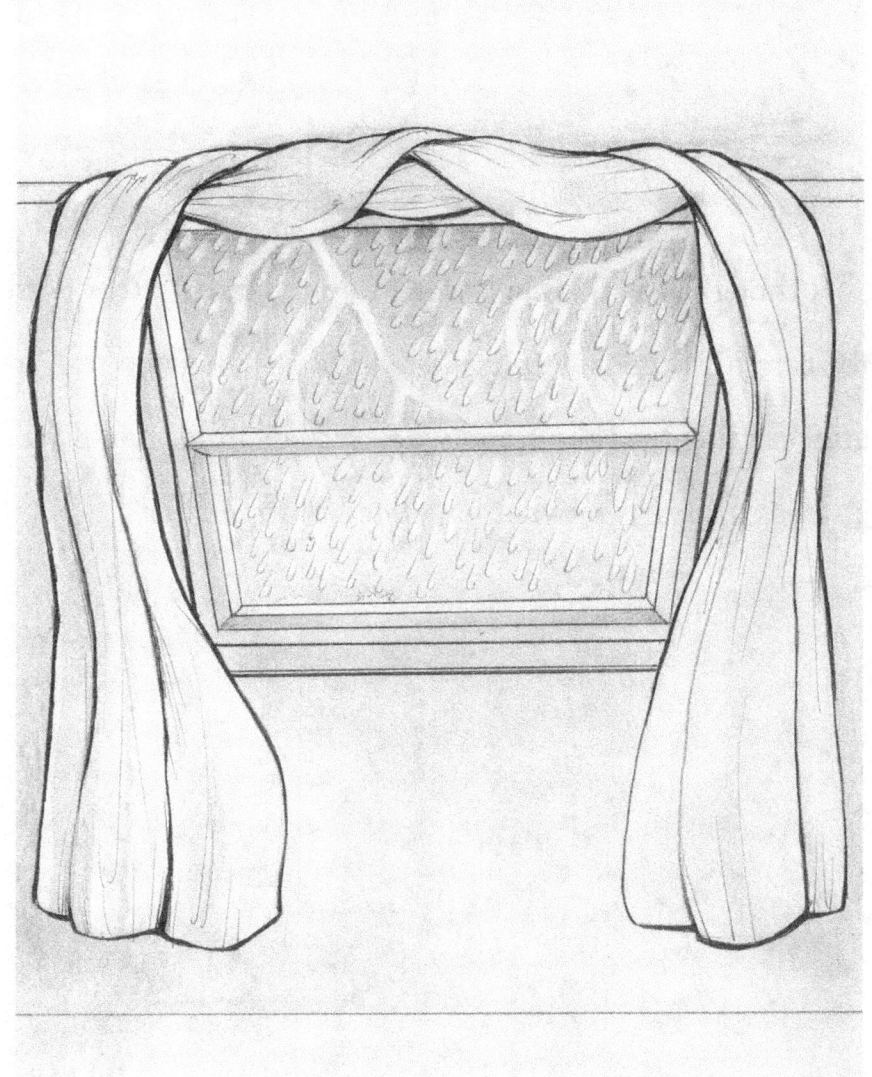

I thought about a Halloween Book that my father used to scare his friends with. But something happened to him after reading that book, and we never saw him again. I was always curious as to what happened to my father.

2

I did not believe in ghosts or monsters; so on the day of my slumber party I went down stairs to the dining room to get the book.

In the mean time Marissa called my friends. She called Andria, Sharon, Kassidy, and Sydney. They were excited and came over immediately. They were dressed in pajamas since it was still a slumber party.

3

We all sat on the bed as I began to read the book. The page before last said do not read the last page, which was page 1,886. But I was curious and turned to page 1,886, the scariest one.

4

In a loud voice we all heard: "You have gone to the highest level; the level that you cannot stop every scary thing that pops."

It will come to you at night when the clock strikes twelve. You will be officially haunted until you find the antidote. Until that time badness will come at you. Be afraid, be very afraid!!

5

The Antidote? Zelda asked while quivering. Yes, the scary voice replied. Your father did not know the antidote, so you will need to find it to save your friends and yourself.

6

"I don't think you should have read that book Zelda," said Marissa, as she and the other girls quivered.

"Would you relax?" Zelda asked, in an annoyed voice.

"You know what happened to your father," said Sydney.

She has a point said Andrea. "Let's just go to sleep." We all

lay down.

7

But then we started talking about scary stuff. When the clock struck twelve we heard noises. Then someone opened the door slowly, down stairs.

My friends, Andrea and Sharon went down stairs to see what caused that sound. They started screaming and tried to run upstairs. But they got pulled back down.

8

Kassidy went down stairs slowly and scarily to see why the girls were making all that noise.

She ran back up stairs huffing and puffing, and so scared that her hairs stood up. She fell as she ran up the stairs. She was nervous and out of breath, as she mumbled, "they have turned white, almost like zombies!!

9

"Don't go down stairs Kassidy pleaded to me and Sydney! She knew that Marissa was too scared to leave the room.

But we wanted to know what happened to Andrea and Sharon; so we went down stairs anyway.

We went into the living room. And behind the closet door stood a big green like creature, a monster, who tried to grab us. But we screamed and ran inside the closet. We hugged each other tightly. Andrea and Sharon had vanished. "I told you, said Sydney!" OK, maybe you were right.

10

Then the big green monster opened the closet door and asked in a creepy voice," why did you read this book to the very end?" You should have stopped before the last page, as the book said. You did not listen.

11

You have a minute to make the antidote. I then said: I wish this was all over. I believe in ghosts and monsters. I want my friends back. I will never read this book again.

Buuut whaaat iiis theee aaantiiidote? The green monster asked loudly and scarily. I will reread the book without going to the last page. I will listen next time.

12

Suddenly Andrea and Sharon had reappeared and turned back to their skin color. He did not harm Sydney or me after I said the antidote. The monster had disappeared and all of us were asleep in the bed.

The next day my father appeared and gave me a book titled "Listen" and a Happy Birthday Balloon!

The End!

AUTHOR'S BIO

I'm a long time employee of the Newark Public School System. I've always loved the art of writing; especially poetry as well as children's stories. I began writing poetry as a way to express my innermost thoughts. Poetry writing became therapeutic for me as a young woman; by helping me deal with the unpleasantries of life. One of my poems "My Face,"was published in "The Voice,"a poetry magazine of the E.O. Library, some decades ago.

My stories are inspired by family; particularly my children. I'm a mother of four and grandmother of two; one of which is Mali-G! The Haunted Book was inspired by my adolescent daughter and Mali-G was inspired by my toddler grandson.

My poetic compilation will be published in the near future; as it will reflect on various aspects of life, including spiritual!

My mottos are "Keep It Going" and "God Is Able."

This book is dedicated to my Daughter Zahria, who is the original author of this story, which I revised and changed most of the names. She wrote the story in the fourth grade for an assignment with open ended questions. She developed the topic into a scary story, and called it "The Haunted Book." I was so fascinated by her imagination that I decided to rewrite it and develop it into a children's fictional story book. Kudos to my young daughter for her vivid imagination!

www.ingramcontent.com/pod-product-compliance
Lightning Source LLC
Chambersburg PA
CBHW071229170626
46809CB00005BA/1996